Where Is the Green Sheep?

Mem Fox and Judy Horacek

Harcourt, Inc.

Orlando   Austin   New York   San Diego   Toronto   London

For Jenny Darling

Requests for permission to make copies of any part of the work should be
mailed to the following address: Permissions Department, Harcourt, Inc.,
6277 Sea Harbor Drive, Orlando, Florida 32887-6777.

www.HarcourtBooks.com

Library of Congress Cataloging-in-Publication Data
Fox, Mem, 1946–
Where is the green sheep?/Mem Fox and Judy Horacek.
p. cm.
Summary: A story about many different sheep, and one that seems to be missing.
[1. Sheep—Fiction. 2. Stories in rhyme.] I. Horacek, Judy. II. Title.
PZ8.3.F8245Gr 2004
[E]—dc21   2003004990
ISBN 0-15-204907-X

First edition
A C E G H F D B

Printed in Singapore

The illustrations in this book were done in Rotring Isograph pens and
Art Stretchers watercolors on Arches hot-press paper.
The display type and text type were set in New Century Schoolbook.
Color separations by Bright Arts Ltd., Hong Kong
Printed and bound by Tien Wah Press, Singapore
This book was printed on totally chlorine-free Stora Enso Matte paper.
Production supervision by Sandra Grebenar and Wendi Taylor
Designed by Scott Piehl

Here is the blue sheep.

And here is the red sheep.

Here is the bath sheep.

And here is the bed sheep.

But where is the
green sheep?

Here is the thin sheep,
and here is the wide sheep.

Here is the swing sheep.

And here is the slide sheep.

But where is the
green sheep?

Here is the up sheep,

and here is the down sheep.

Here is the band sheep.

And here is the clown sheep.

But where is the
green sheep?

Here is the sun sheep.

And here is the rain sheep.

Here is the car sheep,
and here is the train sheep.

But where is the
green sheep?

Here is the wind sheep.

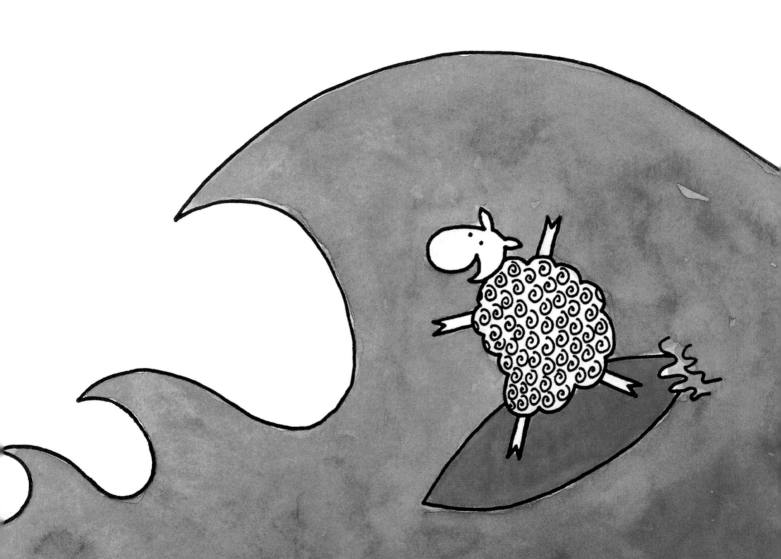

And here is the wave sheep.

Here is the scared sheep,
and here is the brave sheep.

But where is the
green sheep?

Here is the near sheep.

And here is the far sheep.

Here is the moon sheep.

And here is the star sheep.

But where is the
green sheep?

Where IS that
green sheep?

Turn the page quietly—
let's take a peep. . . .

Here's our green sheep,
fast asleep.